The Monsters' Monster

Patrick McDonnell

LITTLE, BROWN AND COMPANY

NEW YORK   BOSTON

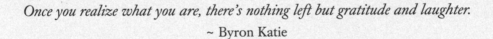

Once you realize what you are, there's nothing left but gratitude and laughter.
~ Byron Katie

To the Big Cheese

Little, Brown and Company • Hachette Book Group • 237 Park Avenue, New York, NY 10017 • Visit our website at www.lb-kids.com

Little, Brown and Company is a division of Hachette Book Group, Inc.

The Little, Brown name and logo are trademarks of Hachette Book Group, Inc.

The publisher is not responsible for websites (or their content) that are not owned by the publisher.

First Edition: September 2012

Library of Congress Cataloging-in-Publication Data

McDonnell, Patrick.   The monsters' monster / Patrick McDonnell. – 1st ed.   p. cm.

Summary: Grouch, Grump, and little Gloom 'n' Doom spend much of their time arguing over who is the "biggest and baddest"

until they build a monster together that turns out to be very different than what they expect.

ISBN 978-0-316-04547-6   [1. Monsters–Fiction. 2. Behavior–Fiction.] I. Title.   PZ7.M1554Mon 2012   [E]–dc23   2011042742

10 9 8 7 6 5 4 3 2 1   SC   Printed in China

Book layout by Jeff Schulz / Menagerie Co.

Grouch, Grump, and little Gloom 'n' Doom
thought they were monsters.

They lived in a dark monster castle,

high atop a dark
monster mountain,

overlooking a monster-fearing village.

Their little monster heads were always filled
with big monster thoughts.

SMASH!

CRASH!!

and

BASH!!!

Huffing and puffing, mad about NOTHING,

their ten favorite words were

and . . .

Every day they argued over who was the
biggest, baddest monster.

Who could complain the loudest?

Who could throw the most
terrible tantrum?

Who was the most miserable?

These debates always
ended in a brawl.

One day they decided to settle the argument once and for all.

Grouch got some tape, tacks, staples, and glue.

Grump found some gunk, gauze, and gobs of goo.

Gloom 'n' Doom grabbed bolts, wire, and a smelly old shoe.

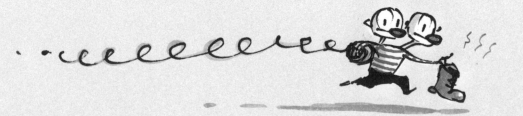

Together they would make a MONSTER monster.
The biggest, baddest monster EVER!

They hoisted their creation into the stormy sky, where

BAM!

A lightning bolt sent a powerful jolt
through the creature.

The monster started to twitch. "He's alive, ALIVE!" the little terrors exclaimed. The monster roared as he stumbled around, tearing away his bandages.

"Big!" little Gloom squealed.

"Bad!!" little Doom squeaked.

"MONSTER!!!" they all cheered together.

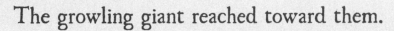

The growling giant reached toward them.

And then, in a deep, booming voice,
he said his first words . . .

He crushed them to his chest
with a tight squeeze.

"Dank you!
Dank you!
Dank you!"

Monster wiggled his stubby monster fingers
and tapped his clunky monster feet.
He looked around in wonder and threw open a window.
The room filled with warm, early dawn light, birdsongs, and dewy, fresh air.

Monster smiled and let out
a little giggle.

"What do you think you're DOING!?!" cried Grouch.

Monster bounced about the room,
gently greeting the many

bats,

rats,

spiders,

and snakes
around him.

"No, no, no, no, NO!!!" shouted the group.

"You're **supposed** to be a MONSTER!"

But Monster didn't think
he was a monster.

He didn't think he was anything . . .

... but thankful to be ALIVE!

Monster became still, sniffing a hint of
sweetness in the morning air.

Suddenly, he let out a ROAR and smashed through the dungeon wall.
"Ha-HA!" Grouch laughed. "He's finally coming to his senses!"
"Yes, yes!!" shouted Grump. "He's off to make mayhem in the village!!"
"He's going to SMASH, CRASH, and BASH!!!" cried Gloom 'n' Doom.

The rascals dashed after Monster, trying to keep up
with his long strides down the mountain.

"MONSTER!

MONSTER!"

they cheered after him.

The village bakery was just opening for the day
when Monster plowed through the front door.

Grouch, Grump, and Gloom 'n' Doom anxiously waited
outside the shop, peering through the dusty windows.

BAKERY

"Big," whispered Gloom.
"Bad," whispered Doom.
"Shh, shh!" begged Grump.
"I want to hear the howls and yowls."

There was a tense quiet, and then finally,
from inside the bakery, they heard . . .

"Dank you!"

Monster appeared,
clutching a white paper bag.

Then he turned and headed
out of town, toward the beach.

"After him!" the trio cried.
"MONSTER! MONSTER!"

Monster slowly knelt down
on the soft, cool sand.

Grouch, Grump, and Gloom 'n' Doom
collapsed in a heap around him.

As they tried to catch their breath,
Monster gently patted their heads.

He carefully opened the bag and gave each of them
a warm, powdered jelly doughnut.

Grouch, Grump, and Gloom 'n' Doom were speechless.

But then they remembered what their big, bad monster had said:

Monster looked at them and smiled. They smiled back.
And together they all started to giggle.

Grouch, Grump, little Gloom 'n' Doom,
and their new friend
sat quietly on the shore,
watching the sunrise . . .

. . . and the seagulls playing . . .

and the sea grass dancing . . .

and the ocean glistening.

And no one was thinking

. . . about being a monster.